Betty Bunny Didn't Do It

Written by Michael B. Kaplan

Illustrated by Stéphane Jorisch

Dial Books for Young Readers
an imprint of Penguin Group (USA) Inc.

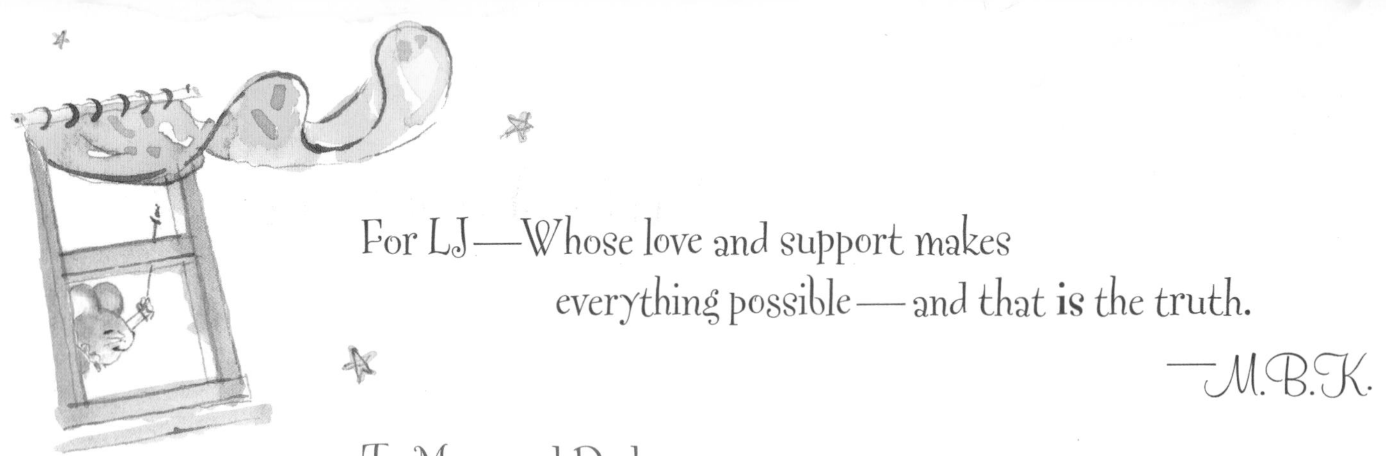

For LJ—Whose love and support makes
everything possible—and that **is** the truth.

—M.B.K.

To Mom and Dad,
who had to deal with my Betty moments

—S.J.

DIAL BOOKS FOR YOUNG READERS • A division of Penguin Young Readers Group
Published by The Penguin Group • Penguin Group (USA) Inc., 375 Hudson Street, New York, NY 10014, U.S.A. • Penguin Group (Canada), 90 Eglinton Avenue East, Suite 700, Toronto, Ontario, Canada M4P 2Y3 (a division of Pearson Penguin Canada Inc.) • Penguin Books Ltd, 80 Strand, London WC2R 0RL, England • Penguin Ireland, 25 St. Stephen's Green, Dublin 2, Ireland (a division of Penguin Books Ltd) • Penguin Group (Australia), 250 Camberwell Road, Camberwell, Victoria 3124, Australia (a division of Pearson Australia Group Pty Ltd) • Penguin Books India Pvt Ltd, 11 Community Centre, Panchsheel Park, New Delhi - 110 017, India • Penguin Group (NZ), 67 Apollo Drive, Rosedale, Auckland 0632, New Zealand (a division of Pearson New Zealand Ltd) • Penguin Books (South Africa) (Pty) Ltd, 24 Sturdee Avenue, Rosebank, Johannesburg 2196, South Africa • Penguin Books Ltd, Registered Offices: 80 Strand, London WC2R 0RL, England

Designed by Jennifer Kelly
Text set in Julius Primary Std
Manufactured in China on acid-free paper

10 9 8 7 6 5 4 3

Library of Congress Cataloging-in-Publication Data
Kaplan, Michael B.
Betty Bunny didn't do it / written by Michael B. Kaplan ; illustrated by Stéphane Jorisch. p. cm.
Summary: When a young rabbit breaks a table lamp and blames the Tooth Fairy, her family explains the importance of honesty.
ISBN 978-0-8037-3858-4 (hardcover)
Special Markets ISBN 978-0-525-42702-5 Not for Resale
[1. Honesty—Fiction. 2. Blame—Fiction. 3. Behavior—Fiction. 4. Family life—Fiction. 5. Rabbits—Fiction.]
I. Jorisch, Stéphane, ill. II. Title. III. Title: Betty Bunny did not do it.
PZ7.K12942Be 2013 [E]—dc23 2012014367

The artwork was rendered on Lanaquarelle watercolor paper in pencil, ink, watercolor, and gouache.

This Imagination Library edition is published by Penguin Young Readers, a division of Penguin Random House, exclusively for Dolly Parton's Imagination Library, a not-for-profit program designed to inspire a love of reading and learning, sponsored in part by The Dollywood Foundation. Penguin's trade editions of this work are available wherever books are sold.

Betty Bunny was a handful.

She knew this because one day she was jumping up and down in her brother Bill's room yelling, "**Play with me!**

Play with me!

Play with me!"

And Bill said, "Man, you're a handful." She knew that she was his favorite sister, so being a handful must be very, very good.

Bill said he was too busy to play with her.

Her brother Henry
and sister Kate were too
busy to play with her.

So Betty Bunny decided to play by herself.

There was no one
to catch the ball.

She threw it anyway.

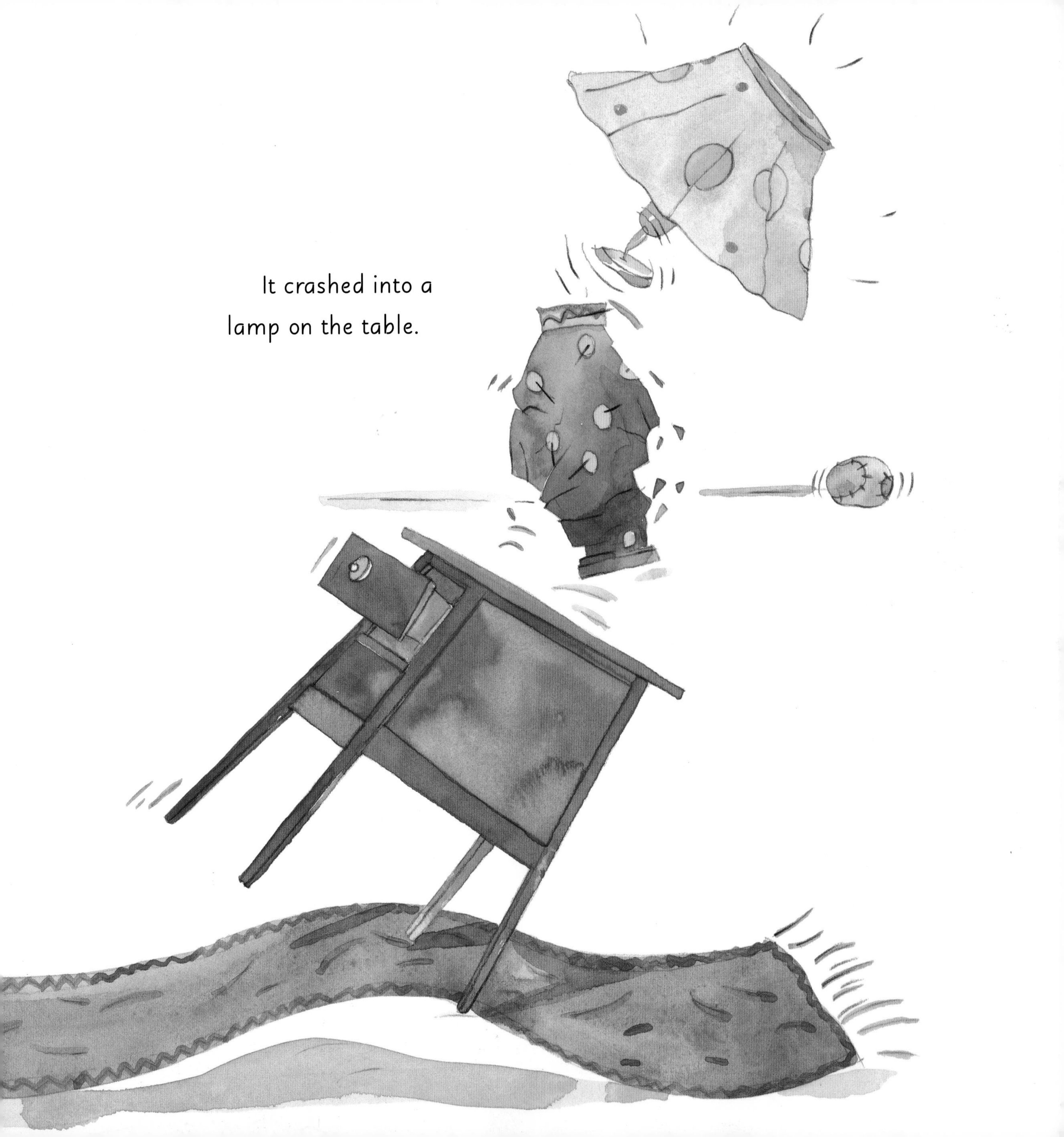

It crashed into a
lamp on the table.

“Oops.”

As Betty Bunny was carefully stuffing the broken lamp under the rug, her brothers and sister came running down the stairs.

"Betty Bunny, I can't believe you broke that lamp," said Henry.

"Let me help you clean it up," said Kate.

"Mom is going to kill you," said Bill. "Forget the lamp. Hide yourself under that rug."

"I didn't do it," Betty Bunny said.

"Then who did?" asked Bill.

Betty Bunny thought about this question for a long time, and then she answered: "The Tooth Fairy."

And Betty Bunny told her brothers and sister all about how the Tooth Fairy had flown into the room and thrown a big bag of baby teeth at the lamp, sending it crashing to the floor.

Blaming someone else for something she had done was such a good idea, Betty Bunny didn't know why she hadn't thought of it before.

"Betty Bunny," Henry said, "you are a **big fat liar**."

Betty Bunny ran into the kitchen screaming, "Mommy, Henry called me fat!"

Betty Bunny's mother was busy making dinner as Henry, Kate, and Bill rushed in. Henry said, "I didn't call her fat. I said she was a big fat liar."

Henry told their mother about how Betty Bunny had broken the lamp and blamed the Tooth Fairy. Now Betty Bunny's mother was very upset. "Betty Bunny, did you break the lamp?"

"No," said Betty Bunny.

"Is that the honest truth?" asked her mother.

"No," said Betty Bunny proudly, "it's an honest lie."

"Betty Bunny, you've never lied to me before," her mother said.

"I know," Betty Bunny said. "It's **new!**"

"Lying is not okay," her mother said. "Why would you do something like that?"

Betty Bunny thought about this question for a long time, and then she answered: "The Tooth Fairy told me to."

And Betty Bunny told her mother all about how the Tooth Fairy had flown into the room and said that if Betty Bunny didn't lie, she would throw a big bag of baby teeth at her.

Her mother said that she had had enough of Betty Bunny's lying. She told Betty Bunny to go straight to her room. When her father got home, they would decide on a punishment.

"You're going to punish the Tooth Fairy?" Betty Bunny asked hopefully.

Her mother shook her head and pointed up the stairs.

As they headed upstairs, Henry said, "Maybe next time you won't do something bad."

Kate said, "Maybe next time you'll tell the truth. We'll still love you."

Bill said, "Maybe next time you'll hide under the rug."

Betty Bunny stopped on the stairs and thought to herself: "Bill is very smart." And so she crawled under the rug to hide from anyone who might be deciding on punishments. She had wriggled her way almost to the center of the rug when she heard a loud CRASH. So she wriggled back out to see what had happened.

And there she saw a broken vase lying on the floor.

Mother, Henry, and Kate came running to see what had made the crashing sound. "I didn't do it," said Betty Bunny, looking at the vase. "I was hiding under the rug."

"Then who did it?" asked her mother. "The Tooth Fairy?"

"Maybe," said Betty Bunny. "I didn't see."

"You just never learn," said Henry.

"You can tell us the truth," said Kate.

"I did it," said Bill, walking in carrying a dust pan and broom. Bill explained how Betty Bunny's ball was on the floor. He tried to toss it into the toy box, but missed and broke the vase.

Mother told Bill that she was very proud of him.

Betty Bunny realized that saying you did something bad made her mother proud. "I broke the lamp!" Betty Bunny said quickly.

She wanted her mother to be **extra**-proud of her, so she also told about the time she drew in crayon on the wall, and the time she ran on the carpet in muddy boots.

She couldn't think of any more bad things, so she made some up, like the time she ate a hundred chocolate cakes before dinner and the time she robbed a bank.

Her mother told Betty Bunny that she was not proud of Bill because he did something bad. She was proud of him for telling the truth. She explained that lying is the worst thing of all, because when you lie, people stop believing you even when you do tell the truth. Just like no one believed Betty Bunny when she said she didn't break the vase.

"That's right. I didn't believe you," said Henry.

"I didn't believe you either," said Kate.

"I still don't believe you, and I know that I did it," said Bill.

Betty Bunny understood. "I will never lie again," she promised.

Her mother was so proud of her that she gave Betty Bunny a **great big hug.**

And Betty Bunny was so proud of herself that when her father came home, she ran to him, calling, "Daddy, Daddy, I'm never going to lie again."

Her father gave her a great big hug too.

Betty Bunny wanted to show how well she could tell the truth, so she said to him, "Daddy, you smell bad."

First her father told her that he just came from the gym and he knew he needed a shower. Then he explained that telling the truth is good, but not if it hurts someone's feelings.

Betty Bunny said that she understood. Then her father noticed the lamp. He was not happy. "What happened here?!" he demanded.

Betty Bunny thought about this question for a long time, and then she answered: "I can't tell you, because it would hurt my feelings."